# Where is that naughty dog?

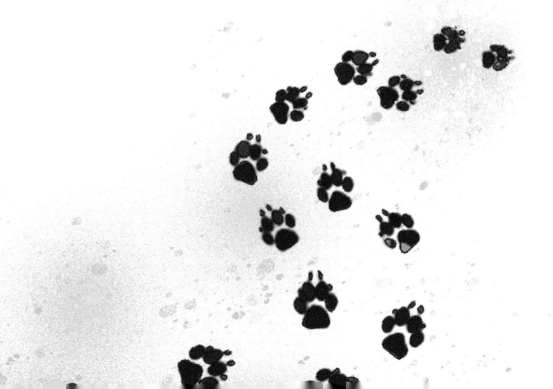

# Where is that naughty dog?

**Sally CL Robinson**

Matador
Unit E2 Airfield Business Park,
Harrison Road, Market Harborough,
Leicestershire. LE16 7UL
Tel: 0116 2792299
Email: books@troubador.co.uk
Web: www.troubador.co.uk/matador
Twitter: @matadorbooks

ISBN 9781 803137 322

British Library Cataloguing in Publication Data.
A catalogue record for this book is available from the British Library.

Typeset in 27pt Grandstander Clean by Troubador Publishing Ltd, Leicester, UK

Matador is an imprint of Troubador Publishing Ltd

For my wonderful husband, who believed in me more than I did myself – I got there eventually! Thank you for persuading me to rescue Captain Chaos with you, otherwise this journey may not have happened – and, of course, the star of the show, Archie with his supporting cast, 'fur' sisters Smiler and Millie.

# This book belongs to

..........................................

Archie is his name,

chaos is his game.

Please can you help me find him?
I saw him running
down the lane.

The problem that we have,
you see, we cannot call him back.

For he is deaf and
cannot hear us.

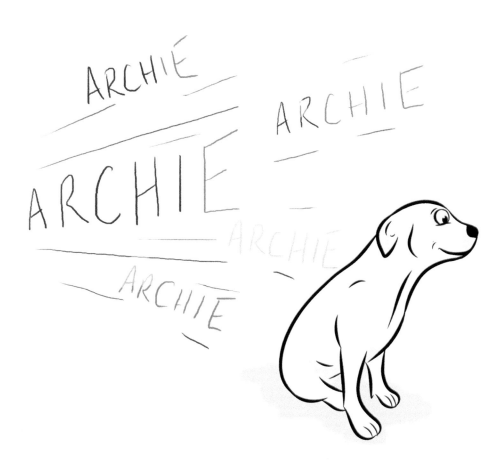

Our job today,

let's track.

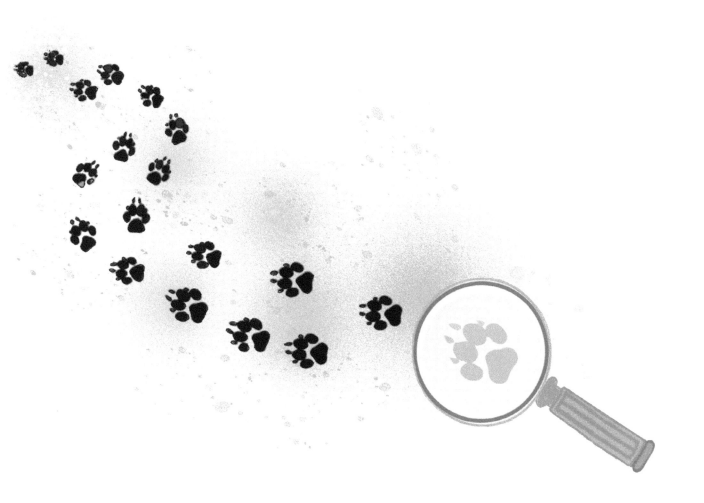

Can you see that bush is rustling?

Do you think he's under there?

No, not him, the ears are way too pointy, so sorry, Mr Hare.

Do you see that bin is moving?

Maybe he's found a bite to eat.

Crikey! That's not him, it's a rat,
that smells like stinky feet!

Is that his tail we saw,

as it slipped behind that tyre?

No, not him, it was a cunning fox with fur as bright as fire.

The sun is going down now,

and night is drawing near.

I worry we won't find him.

He will be all alone, I fear.

Well, it seems his belly started rumbling and he made his own way back.

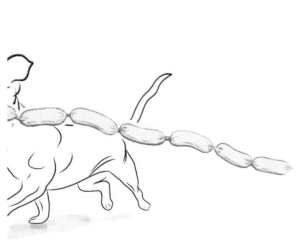

His sense of smell for finding food

is something he doesn't lack.

He's curled up now and sleeping.

Thanks for helping me to track.

Now look, his eyes are peeping,
there's chaos on his mind.

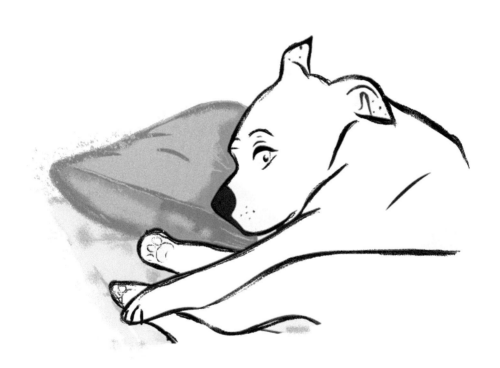

I will be sure to come and get you next time to help me track and seek and find.

BV - #0052 - 010623 - C30 - 216/216/2 - PB - 9781803137322 - Gloss Lamination